THE WHITE SNAKE

Win an exclusive
Gladiator Boy T-shirt and goody bag!

Use the special code below to decode the sentence, then send it in to us.
Each month we will draw one winner to receive a Gladiator Boy T-shirt
and goody bag.

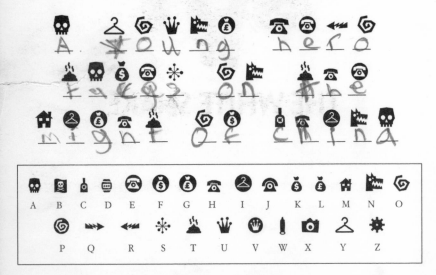

THE WHITE SNAKE

DAVID GRIMSTONE

Hodder
Children's
Books

A division of Hachette Children's Books

First published in Great Britain in 2010
by Hodder Children's Books

A Catalogue record for this book is available from
the British Library

ISBN: 978 0 340 98931 9

Typeset by Tony Fleetwood

Printed and bound in the UK by CPI Bookmarque, Croydon, CR0 4TD

The paper and board used in this paperback by Hodder Children's Books are
natural recyclable products made from wood grown in
sustainable forests. The manufacturing processes conform to the
environmental regulations of the country of origin.

Hodder Children's Books
a division of Hachette Children's Books
338 Euston Road, London NW1 3BH
An Hachette UK company

www.hachette.co.uk

For Chris and Sarah Chapman – you two
ROCK!

This new series is dedicated to Leilani Sparrow,
who has worked tirelessly with Gladiator Boy
since his arrival. Thanks also to Anne McNeil,
who has stood in my corner since day one.

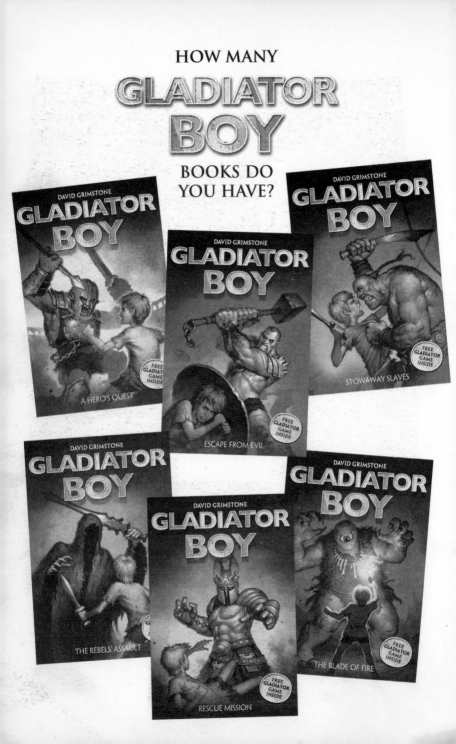

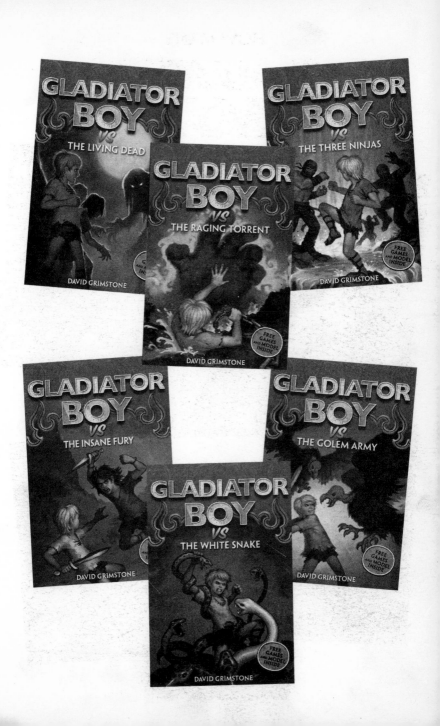

CHINA

PREVIOUSLY IN GLADIATOR BOY

Discovering Teo alive in the dungeons of the Winter Palace, Decimus and his friends rescue the little slave along with another prisoner, the mysterious Princess Akina. However, as they emerge from the depths of the palace dungeons, a grim sight awaits them: the slaves have been betrayed by one of their own. His mind still poisoned by the ninja's red dust, Ruma is swearing that Decimus is now his enemy ... and has declared war on his former friends. The battle in the east goes on ...

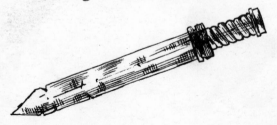

CHAPTER
I

CHARGE!

The sky turned black, and two heavy rumbles of thunder announced the arrival of what was to be an incredibly violent storm. In the gardens of the Winter Palace, an even more violent tempest was taking place ...

Ruma ran towards Decimus Rex with a whirlwind of anger raging inside him. A fire flashed in his dark eyes, warning the young gladiator that he would not show him the slightest mercy.

Decimus prepared himself for the onslaught, but a very different emotion wrestled for control in his mind: regret. Ruma wasn't himself – something had happened to him, and Decimus wanted to know what it was ... preferably before his

friend was completely lost to him.

All around the pair, a frenzied war was taking place. Slavious Doom's guards had poured on to the field, led by two of King D'Tong's surviving ninjas. They had been met with terrible force by Gladius, Argon, Olu and Teo, all determined to fight them to the death. The odds should have been against the slaves, but Princess Akina was fighting with enough skill for ten men. She catapulted between the guards with lightning speed, avoiding every attempted lunge, and hit both ninjas with a single spinning kick that sent the pair crashing to the ground.

Ruma charged into Decimus with all his might, but the young gladiator crouched slightly, using the Etrurian's own weight to send him hurtling over his back and on to the floor. Ruma hit the ground hard, but barely seemed to notice. He was back on his feet so quickly that Decimus had no time to prepare another move before he'd been caught with a backhand that knocked him sideways. He staggered slightly, blocked two more of Ruma's blows and then delivered one of his own: an elbow driven upwards with enough force to stun the Etrurian for a few seconds at least.

Ruma shook his head slightly, and Decimus made a deliberate step back.

'It's ME, Ruma! Decimus! Your FRIEND! Think about what you're— ooof!'

Ruma cannoned into the young gladiator, and they both fell to the ground, rolling over one another in an attempt to land the first solid punch of the fight.

Gladius, in the meantime, had choked one guard into unconsciousness and, having robbed the man of his helmet, was now using the armour to strike some damaging blows against several of the others. Beside him, Teo was fighting with the sort of ferocity that would never have been expected from a boy who'd been manacled in a cage for over a year. The little prisoner was punching, kicking, biting and spitting at a large guard who was evidently not prepared for such a spirited opponent.

Argon had his own victim well outmatched: using his immense strength to wrench the man off his feet, he hurled him like a cannonball at three others, who went down like a line of skittles. Olu had opted to help Princess Akina in her assault on the ninjas, but he arrived at her side to discover that his assistance would not be needed: the feisty royal had rendered both her enemies unconscious with some sort of snake-like death-grip that made Olu glad he was on her side.

Decimus had fought many opponents in his life, but he'd always been wary of Ruma. Although they'd grown to be friends in the

Arena, he'd regularly feared that they might one
day have to face each other.

The wiry Etrurian had taken just about
everything Decimus had; every crafty strike,
every disguised punch, every finishing sweep . . .
and he was still standing. Moreover, Decimus

17

was becoming tired; tired and desperate to end the conflict quickly.

He threw out a fist that caught Ruma on the side of the head, but as he moved in to follow up on the move he tripped, and was immediately ensnared in a headlock: the Etrurian crunched down with all his might.

'You're weak, Decimus, did you know that?' he snarled. 'Oh, you're clever, and you fight well ... but you haven't ... got the stamina ... for ... combat.'

He gritted his teeth with the effort of maintaining the hold, spit dripping from his lips, he felt the young gladiator begin to fight back.

Decimus let out a pained cry that seemed to be half-fury, half-anguish. Then he lifted Ruma bodily off the ground and simply hurled him in a random direction. The Etrurian flew over the heads of two struggling combatants and landed on top of the prone ninjas. He quickly staggered to his feet, but fell down again, evidently dazed and shocked at the strength Decimus had managed to summon against him.

On the battlefield, Gladius had stopped fighting. He had nailed several guards with his newly acquired helmet, but was now focusing with no small amount of terror on the new set of guards Doom was sending towards them. It wasn't so much that they seemed particularly fierce or well-armoured, but that there were so many of them. This fight was hopeless. Completely hopele—

Gladius dropped the helmet, and it hit the ground just a few seconds before his jaw fell open in complete amazement.

A new, impossibly huge figure was advancing on the battlefield. It moved in an awkward sort of stride, as if it had seen people walking around but couldn't quite work out how it was done. Gladius thought of the figure as an 'it', though it was obviously male – there were muscles and veins and horrible, horrible scars all over its immense bulk. The sight was just astonishing. Argon had muscles, in a way that suggested he'd done lots of exercise and heavy lifting; this thing had muscles as if it had been *made* from them: sacks and sacks of them all crowded together, networked by pulsing veins and scars that were all red raw. It was the ugliest human he'd ever seen in his life, and that was without seeing its face: thankfully, a black mask covered the thing's actual features – the only piece of cloth on the beast save for a torn loin-rag that barely covered its midsection.

The others hadn't seen it.

Gladius opened his mouth to scream out a warning, but he couldn't make himself heard above the frenzy of the battle.

Instead, he did the only thing he could do in order to save his friends from such a terrible threat – he charged it.

The slaves had cleared the battlefield. Stepping over guard after guard, they gathered together: Akina allowed herself a small smile of satisfaction as Teo, Argon and Olu all glanced at her handiwork with the ninjas, amazed at the unexpected warrior who had come into their midst. They felt considerably fortunate to be in her company, until a sudden, deathly silence caused them all to turn slowly around.

Three things were happening on the battlefield simultaneously. First, Decimus and Ruma were locked in a grim test of strength at the end of which one of them would undoubtedly be forced to their knees. At the moment, the struggle looked like it might go either way, but Decimus had the sort of determined stance that had won him so many trials at the arena.

Slavious Doom was standing to one side of the action, his hand raised in a gesture that had caused his new guard troop to pause in their approach.

Instead, the gang stood silently, their eyes fixed on the two slaves.

Doom's own gaze, however, was elsewhere.

Across the field, raised in the air like a rag doll, was Gladius, kicking frantically at the *thing* that had one hand clamped around his throat. One, single hand was holding him aloft, effortlessly.

Olu, Teo and Akina all stared, open-mouthed, at the brutish nightmare on the far side of the field ... but Argon got himself together with remarkable speed. Snatching a heavy shield from the ground beside the heap of unconscious guards, the muscular Gaul dashed across the field towards the scene of the combat, where Gladius was evidently beginning to tire. The big slave's body was almost limp, his legs kicking out once or twice to no avail.

Finally, the others realized the gravity of the situation and began to hurry after Argon, but the Gaul was way ahead of them. Skidding to a halt and moving around behind the beast, Argon heaved the great shield above him and brought it crashing with all his might against

24

the giant's back.

Once.

Twice.

On the third strike, the resulting noise was so great that it caused all the slaves to stop in their tracks.

Even Decimus, locked in a deadly struggle against Ruma, momentarily broke eye contact with the Etrurian in order to see what had made the din.

Yet, despite a series of terrible welts on the grotesque back of the thing, it still made no sign of even having *noticed* the attack. Gladius was now choking to death.

Decimus tried to grit his teeth in an effort to break Ruma down and win his struggle, but his mind was on Gladius . . . and, because of this, the Etrurian was beginning to overpower him.

Acting almost on instinct instead of conscious thought, Decimus did the one thing he knew Ruma wouldn't be expecting him to do: he dropped to his knees.

Making a deliberate show of losing his strength, Decimus folded up beneath Ruma, but in doing so he drove his head hard into the wiry Etrurian's stomach. As if this wasn't enough to double the slave over, Decimus then thrust up a palm ... and knocked his opponent out cold.

A round of sudden applause shook him from his reverie, and he locked eyes with Slavious Doom for the first time.

'Good! GOOD!' the overlord boomed. 'I

knew he would be no match for you, my young friend. But the combat was *so* interesting to watch.' Waving a hand towards Argon, who was *still* using the shield as a battering ram to no avail, he smiled once more.

'I see you've come to look upon my new apprentice. I call him GROACH. As you can see, he is a vast improvement upon the late Drin Hain. He will also KILL your friend in but a few seconds unless you and your pathetic band surrender IMMEDIATELY.'

Decimus felt the blood rising in his veins, but he wasn't stupid – Ruma had taken a lot out of him and, besides, if Argon couldn't damage this beast with a great brass shield, what could he possibly hope to achieve with just his bare hands or even, he ventured, a sword? Besides, they'd already felt the pain of losing *one* friend ... could they really welcome Teo's return only to end up grieving after Gladius?

Not this time. A single glance at the others told Decimus that his thoughts were shared, and he reluctantly stepped away from Ruma, his hands thrust in the air.

'Excellent! Excellent!' Doom shouted, his voice almost dripping with glee. He turned slightly and yelled at his new henchman. 'Groach! Let him go.'

There were a few seconds of silence, during which even Doom looked momentarily concerned.

'GROACH! Let him go NOW!'

The command was finally acknowledged, and Gladius was dropped to the ground like a sack of potatoes. Argon rushed over to help him, while a team of Doom's guards began to chain up the remaining friends.

Even as a short, stocky guard tied his hands behind his back, Decimus still glared at the imposing figure of Slavious Doom.

'Let the princess free,' the overlord shouted. 'She is D'Tong's prisoner ... and that weak fool has done nothing to deserve my allegiance. You –' Doom turned to glance at Teo, as the princess took several surprised steps away from the guards, '– have also served my purpose: it was worth the effort of saving your life, of pumping the air back into those tiny lungs ... just to entrap your stupid friends once again. Haahahaha!'

Teo looked defiant; the little prisoner made no move to step away from his companions.

'She deserve go,' he said, smiling at Akina as he conveyed Doom's decision to her in their own language. The princess was obviously desperate to return to her father: her eyes filled with tears.

'Not me,' Teo said, finally. 'I stay.'

'It is your choice,' Doom snarled. 'Go free in your own land . . . or suffer the same fate as your friends.'

Decimus gave Teo a warning glare, but it was completely ignored. The little slave, it seemed, had made his decision.

'What do you want from me, Doom?' Decimus shouted, as the guards began to haul the others away. 'You wouldn't have gone to all this trouble just to kill me – you could have done that at home! So what is it this time that you haven't got the courage to do yourself? Wrestle a god? Break down a mountain? Swallow poison?'

Slavious Doom turned to walk away from the field, but slowly glanced back over his shoulder.

'You will find out, Decimus Rex,' he laughed. 'You will find out soon enough. I will only say that I never truly expected you to die in the water maze – you are one of life's *born survivors, my young friend.* Those ninjas of D'Tong's were no match for you either ... they were merely ... a test. Hahahaha!'

CHAPTER
II

PIN YON
ROCK

Decimus Rex had been unconscious for the best part of a day. When he *did* finally awake, he was immediately plunged into a grim world of vague shadows and stinking flesh.

The room he found himself in was actually a large cage, and he knew from experience that he was on the bilge deck of a large ship. An empty bucket slid back and forth across the floor beyond the bars, and a stack of rotten-looking barrels rocked steadily with the rise and fall of the ocean. Two heavy lanterns had been chained to the top of the cage, but they were both encased in grime and neither threw out much light.

Decimus slowly gazed at his surroundings, and noticed his friends for the first time. Argon,

Teo and Olu were all still unconscious; only Gladius was awake, and *he* was being sick in the corner of the enormous cage.

Decimus took a deep breath, and tried to hold it in as long as possible – the smell from the deck was indescribable.

Dragging himself up by the bars, he managed

to work his way over to the rough wooden bench that sprouted from the near wall. He took several further breaths, and then tried to clear his head.

'G-Gladius,' he muttered. 'Wh-what happened?'

Gladius looked up, one hand wiping the moisture from his lips. 'You mean after that monster almost choked me to death?' he said, weakly.

'Yeah . . . after that.'

'Doom's men clubbed us all out. This must be his ship – we're probably on our way back to Rome.'

Decimus shook his head, vehemently.

'No, we're not,' he said, his face set in a grimace. 'Whatever Doom is searching for, it's definitely out *here* somewhere.'

'You think?'

'I KNOW him, Gladius. I know the way he thinks – this whole trap with Teo, the trouble of getting us to travel here – it's all been about using us to find another one of his legendary obsessions.'

'You mean – like the Blade of Fire?'

'Exactly.'

'But how can you be sure—'

'Isn't it obvious? We're all still alive, aren't we? Besides that, we've faced everything he's ever thrown at us . . . and that means we're the best weapon he's got!'

Olu began to murmur, and shifted slightly as his eyelids flickered in the half-light. Decimus and Gladius both hurried over to help their friend to his feet. Beside them, Argon and Teo were also stirring.

'Where's Ruma?' Olu said, when he managed to right himself.

'Who cares?' Gladius spat. 'He betrayed us all and tried to kill Decimus!'

'Yeah,' Olu conceded. 'But you know why, don't you? The red dust! We still don't know how badly it mangled his mind!'

'I hope he's OK,' Decimus admitted, crouching to help Argon and Teo as both regained consciousness.

As the friends all tried to help one another gain their footing in the cage, the trapdoor to the deck above flew open and a series of burly Roman guards scrambled down the ladder and dropped on to the floor. They were followed, at length, by Slavious Doom himself. Groach was nowhere to be seen, presumably – Decimus thought – because his vast expanse wouldn't fit through the hatch.

'Good!' Doom bellowed. 'You are all awake. What excellent fortune – we have just arrived at our destination.'

The overlord took several steps towards the cage, and glared in at Decimus Rex.

'Take them up on deck,' he growled. 'They deserve to see the task ahead of them.'

'Unless this *task* involves me plunging a dagger into your worthless corpse,' Decimus growled, 'you might as well leave me to rot in this prison: I will do nothing more for you.'

Doom merely smiled, and gave the order for

the prisoners to be dragged from the cage.

The ship rocked gently on the calm ocean waters as the slaves were paraded on to the deck. The morning sun beat down on them all, impossibly bright in contrast to the murky gloom from which they had emerged.

As Decimus stepped into the light, he saw line after line of Roman guards standing around the deck, all muttering to one another and smirking in his general direction. There was no sign of Ruma.

In the middle of the deck stood Slavious Doom, but the giant overlord was almost completely eclipsed by the monstrous form of Groach, who occupied the shade behind him.

The wall of vein-scarred muscle shifted a few times as the beast slowly folded its arms, but the masked face remained completely still, causing Decimus to wonder if the henchman even breathed the same air as he did.

Slavious Doom waited for his men to arrange Teo, Argon, Olu and Gladius in a line beside Decimus, and then he pointed east.

'Allow me to welcome you to Pin Yon Rock,' he growled. 'Home of the legendary White Snake of Zheen. Feast your eyes.'

Almost as one, the slaves looked out toward the land mass that occupied the entire view from the port side of the ship.

Pin Yon Rock was exactly that – an enormous jut of rock that appeared to be a half-formed island. There were trees dotted around the

mass, and several craggy paths that led to the single dominating feature: a solid-looking fortress that actually seemed to grow out of the rock it occupied, its lone tower reaching for the sky like a gnarled finger.

It was then that Decimus noticed the army. Camped on the various paths and outcrops all over Pin Yon Rock were horde after horde of guards, all bearing the seal of Slavious Doom.

A look of confusion settled on the young gladiator's face, but Doom spoke before he could muster the question.

'Yes,' the overlord boomed. 'I want what is inside, and I am determined to get it. We have had the entire island under siege for the last six months. No one comes out . . .'

'. . . but you can't get in!' Decimus almost

laughed as he finished Doom's sentence. 'I'm thinking you've already tried a full-on attack, so now you're completely failing to starve them out. Six months, eh? Ha! You must be a laughing stock by now!'

A terrible silence settled on the deck as Doom's features began to crease with a furious, uncontrollable anger.

'I did not bring you here to suffer further humiliations brought on by your poisoned *mouth*,' he screamed. 'Tomorrow morning, at dawn, you will get *inside* the fortress, kill the handful of guards that still remain and capture the White Snake itself. If you refuse, Groach will strangle your friends in front of you, one by one ... and, this time, no effort will be made to revive them.'

Doom allowed himself a smile, as a chorus of sniggers erupted all around him. Then, as Decimus looked on with mounting anger, several guards rushed forward and began to drag Gladius and Argon back to the far side of the deck.

Decimus, Olu and Teo all tried to intercept their friends as they were hauled apart, but the guards were too many and they soon found themselves forced on to their knees.

'Why them?' Olu shouted. 'Why take Gladius and Argon? Why not me? Or Teo?'

Doom grinned broadly, and this time his eyes flashed with a flare of evil malice that Decimus had come to recognize.

'Let us simply say that they are not *suitable* for the mission and leave it at that. It is *their* lives you will forfeit if you fail to complete the task. Guards! Take them below – they deserve one small meal before their moment of glory!'

A roar of diabolical laughter echoed around the ship as Decimus, Olu and Teo were dragged back to the bilge deck.

Midnight arrived, and a full moon illuminated the deck of the ship. Outlined against the shadows, a single diminutive figure emerged from a tiny crawlspace beside the captain's cabin and crept across the boards. It stopped several times, very careful not to reveal itself to the handful of guards who had stayed up late to keep a lookout, before proceeding to the underdecks.

When the figure reached the first hatch, it gently lifted the trapdoor and lowered itself down . . .

. . . and down . . .

. . . and down.

When it arrived on the bilge deck, the figure dropped on to all fours and crawled across the floor, all the while keeping to the shadows cast by the lantern-light.

The guard on duty heard nothing, and remained dozing even as the figure brought a heavy iron bowl down on the back of his head. He grunted slightly, and slid off the stool he'd been occupying.

Despite the noise of the clunk and the resulting grunt, the slaves in the deck-cell remained in a deep sleep.

Only Decimus was wide awake. He couldn't see the face of the figure in the shadows, but he didn't really need to.

48

'I wondered when you would show up,' he muttered.

'Decimus ... I'm SO sorry.'

Ruma emerged from the gloom. As he moved towards the cage, Decimus saw that his face looked exceptionally drawn and lined, but the glow in his eyes had vanished.

'Doom has me scrubbing the decks,' he whispered. 'He promised to let me live, as long as I help him to kill you when the time comes.'

The young gladiator smiled. 'When I've fetched the White Snake, you mean?'

'Yeah,' said the Etrurian, with a distracted nod. Suddenly, he looked about ready to cry. 'I don't feel controlled any more,' he said. 'I don't feel the anger. I just feel ... ashamed. That stuff made me think *you* were the evil one! All I could see was blood and death! Now, I'm just pretending to hate you because I don't know what else to do. I'm SO sorry . . . please forgive m—'

Decimus reached through the bars with lightning speed and snatched hold of Ruma, dragging the Etrurian forward so that their faces were mere inches apart.

'You *swear* to me you're telling the truth?' he snarled, his eyes burning into Ruma's face. 'You *swear* he hasn't sent you down here to force me into another trap? SWEAR it, Ruma – look at me and SWEAR it.'

Ruma nodded, tears streaming down his face.

'I swear!' he said, and then the words all came out in a rush. 'I listened to him telling

his men everything! He wants you to swim

through this tiny hole that's underneath the rock

– that's why he wanted to test you in the water maze! He never thought for one second that you would actually die: it was ALL for this. He thinks Teo and Olu will make it because they're small, but he knows only you can defeat the warriors who are waiting inside the fort!'

Decimus allowed his wretched friend to talk until he was near exhaustion. Then, finally, he released Ruma from the vice-like grip he'd had on him.

'You are forgiven,' he growled. 'But if you don't help me get the key to this cell right now, the others might not be around to do the same!'

Ruma staggered back from the bars, a look of sudden determination on his weathered face. Then he hurried off in to the shadows once more.

Decimus turned to his sleeping companions, and gently shook them awake.

CHAPTER III

ABANDON SHIP!

For a long time, Decimus genuinely thought that Ruma would not return. He was wrong, however, and the Etrurian eventually reappeared. He looked frightened and very weary, but he was holding a bunch of keys.

This time, both Olu and Teo were ready to move. Of course, they still had to find the others, but this was certainly a very good start.

The ship lurched suddenly on a strong wave, but quickly settled again.

It was only as Ruma was carefully unlocking the cell door that Decimus saw the worried look in his eyes.

'Did you have to sneak into Doom's quarters to get the key?' he muttered.

The Etrurian shook his head. 'If I could

sneak into Doom's quarters any time I wanted, I probably would have strangled the evil wretch by now. No, he's very well guarded – snatching the keys, on the other hand, was easy.'

'Then why do you look so worried?' Olu interrupted; he had also noticed the pained look on Ruma's face, and was concerned. 'You're not still under the influence of that powder, surel—'

'No!' the Etrurian snapped. 'If I *was*, I wouldn't be here – I'm upset because we don't have a *hope* of rescuing Argon and Gladius, OK? They're being guarded by Groach in a cabin at the top of the ship . . . and the monster's wide awake.'

The cabin was actually more of a large, square

space hollowed out at the back of one of the lower decks. There were no bars or cell-sections visible, but Decimus soon saw that no such precautions were needed: Groach was more than enough to ensure the slaves remained where they were.

The beast was simply standing in the middle of the room, glaring down at the two unconscious prisoners in his care. Decimus was surprised to see that Groach still had his mask on, and wondered what kind of horrors required concealing even in the dead of night.

Gladius and Argon showed no signs of having been attacked or brutalized in any way, which came as another surprise to Decimus ... especially since Doom had needed to shout twice before Groach had released his chokehold

on Gladius during the battle. A large iron mace

lay on the floor between them, presumably as a

temptation to engage Groach in some sort of

pointless combat.

'What do we do?' Olu whispered, as he and

Teo crouched in the dark behind Decimus.

'Argon tried three times to knock that monster out . . . and he was using a *brass shield*. You shouldn't have asked Ruma to keep lookout – we need to hit this thing with *force*.'

Decimus turned to his friend in the shadows, and cupped a hand over his mouth in order to stifle his own ragged voice.

'Are you faster than Teo?' he whispered.

Olu glanced sideways at the little slave, who seemed to understand the question but apparently had no strong opinion on the subject.

'No,' Olu concluded, shaking his head. 'I think he has the edge on me – why? What's the plan?'

Decimus leaned in close to Teo, and used a number of careful gestures to enhance his

60

instructions, so as to cross the language barrier.

'Teo – can you get that *thing's* attention and then evade him? Hmm ... evade ... er ... run *around* him, like this?'

Decimus made circles with his hands and pointed at Groach.

'Yes,' Teo muttered. 'I do.'

Without another word, the little slave darted forward and – to their horror – slapped Groach hard across the small of his back.

Neither Decimus nor Olu had been expecting Teo to act so quickly, or in such a straightforward manner – and it soon turned out that Groach was equally surprised. The scarred giant glanced around at his back, as if looking for an insect to swat, but Teo was already underneath him. The little slave slashed his long fingers across the back of Groach's leg and quickly rolled aside, just as the monster dropped into a crouch and drove a fist *through* the floor of the deck.

The noise caused Gladius and Argon to awake with such a start that they actually clashed heads, and Decimus imagined it had probably woken half the ship in the process.

'Out! Now!' he screamed, rushing forward to help the dazed pair on to their feet.

Then Groach caught hold of Teo. It happened so quickly that Olu, watching from the doorway, gasped with surprise. The beast had thrown out an arm with remarkable speed, and had snatched the little slave up as if he was grabbing a rat. Almost without pause, he hurled Teo across the length of the room and sent him

crashing into a wood-pile that quickly

collapsed upon impact.

Decimus didn't have to check if his friend

was hurt; the agonized cry Teo made as he hit

63

the wood told him everything he needed to know.

In a maddened response to the act, Argon rushed forward and punched Groach with all his might. The resulting blow was one Decimus was certain would have knocked *him* about twenty feet in the air.

Groach didn't budge. He simply growled in annoyance, slapped a hand around Argon's neck and lifted him bodily off the deck. Then, in several swift steps, he crossed the room and deposited the Gaul on top of Teo with a sickening thud.

Everything was going wrong.

'Doom's men are coming! Get out! Get out NOOOWW!'

The cry had come from Ruma, who hurtled

through the door at the end of the deck with a frantic edge to his cries.

Sensing that their chance of escape was ebbing away, Decimus did something he would never otherwise have considered. He turned on his heel and fled. 'Everyone run! Ruuuuuuuuuun!'

Olu made to dash after him, but a wooden plank glanced off his head and dropped him like a sack of potatoes. He was still attempting to scramble on to his feet when Groach, having successfully hit him with *one* throw, immediately followed with another. This time the hurled plank slammed Olu full in the face, knocking him out instantly.

Decimus and Ruma hurtled out of the cabin. 'Ruuuunnn!'

Groach grunted with satisfaction, and turned toward the two retreating slaves in order to give chase.

Then he staggered back: the mace had hit him with so much weight behind it that, for a second, it actually looked as though the beast was going down.

Gladius gulped, raised the mace nervously for

a second strike . . . and hit the floor, hard.

In his dizzy state, Groach evidently hadn't been able to tell where the mace had come from . . . so he'd guessed. A single, sweeping punch had blasted Gladius into unconsciousness.

Groach shook his head to dislodge the buzz that now echoed in his ears, and hurried after the escaped slaves.

'Abandon ship! Abandon ship!'

Ruma charged for the port side of the deck, his attempts at causing confusion among the arriving guards thwarted when Decimus exploded from the cabin behind him.

Two burly Romans attempted to halt the Etrurian's dash, but Ruma was way ahead of them.

Avoiding the first lunge and glancing aside the second, he then snatched a heavy-looking winch from a nearby barrel-top and began to mindlessly batter his way to the edge of the deck. Before a second wave of guards could reach him, there was a blur of activity, followed by a distant splash.

Decimus didn't waste any time, either. He tore along the path Ruma had ripped open for him, determined not to get caught up in any fight that might delay him making his escape.

As he shoved aside the only guard that stood between him and the shifting ocean, he felt a momentary pang of terrible guilt.

He had abandoned his friends, possibly to a grim fate. What sort of fool would do such a thing?

Decimus leapt over the edge of the deck and

plummeted into the waters far below. As he hit the waves and entered the dark and murky world of shadows beneath the bulk of the ship, a new determination settled his mind.

He might be escaping, but he was escaping with a plan ... and, if it worked, Slavious Doom would not dare harm any of his friends.

CHAPTER IV

BITTEN

Ruma was no stranger to water, but swimming in the ocean was very different to swimming anywhere else. Perhaps it was the knowledge that the world he'd entered was so incredibly vast, or that it contained so many dangerous and wild creatures. The only thing keeping him from re-surfacing was the fact that Doom would undoubtedly have his men in tiny boats, trawling around the ship and searching for any sign that they might still be within grabbing distance.

And then there was Decimus.

The young gladiator made another turn in the water, and kicked his legs with renewed effort.

Decimus was swimming beneath the waves

with a resolve that had to be the result of prior knowledge. Ruma was certain that his friend had never been in these waters before, yet he appeared to know exactly where he was heading ... and even the Etrurian could tell they were cutting a direct path *towards* Pin Yon Rock.

A direction that was surely madness?

When the young gladiator finally *did* go up for air, Ruma immediately followed him, snatching his arm as they both broke the

crest of the water.

'Where are you going?' the Etrurian spat, glancing back at Doom's ship, which had become a hive of activity in the distance. 'Not *to* the Rock, surely? Doom has over a hundred men camped out up there!'

Decimus shook his head, and smiled.

'You told me how Doom expected us to get into the fort, remember?'

The Etrurian nodded. 'Of course; through the tiny hole under the rock.'

'Did you see any plans; any hint of where it might be?'

Ruma shook his head. 'No, but his captain mentioned the south side, near the back of the fort.'

'Let's go, then.'

'We're going to do what Doom *wants*?'

Decimus shook his head.

'No,' he said, defiantly. 'We're not.'

Then he dived beneath the water, once again.

It took them many, many attempts to find the secret entrance to the fort. Decimus wasn't certain how much time they'd wasted in the shallows around the Rock, but the sun had been up when he'd last surfaced for air … so he guessed they'd been off the ship for at least six or seven hours.

Eventually, Ruma had found an underwater cave with an entrance so tiny and narrow that it had required three separate efforts to enter … and even then they only *just* managed it.

Narrowly avoiding a family of vicious-looking eels that had congregated near the back of the cave, Decimus and Ruma splashed up out of the water and rolled on to the foot of a dark, dank stairway that had been hollowed out of the rock itself. Seaweed glistened on the craggy walls and the only sound was that of the water lapping against the steps.

'What are we doing here, exactly?' Ruma spluttered, forcing himself up on to his elbows.

Decimus nodded towards the stairwell, and dragged himself on to his feet. 'Isn't it obvious?' he said, with a cryptic smile. 'We're going to get Doom's precious White Snake.'

The stone stairway seemed to meander on forever, twisting and turning several times but never once looking as though it was about to end at a door or an archway.

Decimus sighed as he waited for Ruma to catch up with him, and trudged on. The Etrurian had been counting each and every step, and announced that there were six hundred and twenty-five, so far.

However, the young gladiator wasn't listening – he was too busy focusing on a distant green glow that appeared to be coming from a point halfway up the next flight.

Motioning to Ruma to be very careful, he suddenly leapt up the remaining steps and stared off down this new junction.

The green glow was coming from a strangely luminous slime that grew on the walls of the passage beyond, which looked like a mini sewer tunnel. There was also a crude iron ladder fixed to one wall; it led to a disc-shaped plate in the ceiling.

'If this goes to the fort,' Ruma whispered, 'why do the stairs continue?'

Decimus thought for a moment, and seemed

to come to a conclusion.

'The fort's main tower is actually part of the rock,' he said. 'So I reckon the stairs go to the top of the tower, while *this* way leads into the fort itself. Let's find out if I'm right.' He paused, adding: 'Keep away from that slime, though – I don't like the look of it, much.'

Ruma nodded, and the two friends made for the iron ladder.

It took a lot of effort, but eventually the plate shifted and Decimus was able to shoulder it out of its niche. The disc clattered aside, loudly, revealing what appeared to be a small courtyard inside the fort.

Decimus winced when he heard the noise

they'd made, and was about to curse their lack of stealth when he realized that there wasn't anyone around to hear them: the place was completely abandoned. At least, it *seemed to be*.

He clambered out of the hole and dragged Ruma after him. Together, the pair glanced around at the empty interior of the fort.

The courtyard contained several exits, but doors were hanging off their hinges in every direction. Either there had been a major battle in this fort, or else the inhabitants had left in a *big* hurry. The two towering double doors were barred from the inside, however, and had obviously proved completely impenetrable.

A number of skilfully carved statues were dotted around the various doorways, but many of these were chipped or broken and several were even missing limbs. The whole place was quite a depressing sight.

Decimus snatched up a rusty-looking sword that had been carelessly discarded on the rough cobbles, and Ruma soon found a near-identical weapon in another corner of the courtyard.

Then they began to explore the fort.

'This doesn't make sense,' Ruma whispered. 'If Doom's men had been in here, already, they wouldn't still be camped outside . . . and the people here can't have left because Doom would have seen them.'

Ruma nodded. 'This place gives me the creeps.'

They entered one of the doors and moved through several rooms, each one more curious and empty than the last.

'I think these people made statues,' Ruma muttered, noticing another collection of the broken sculptures in a chamber that looked as though it had once been a kitchen of some sort. 'They probably sold them on the mainland for piles and piles of gold – the detail is amazing. AND there are hundreds of them!'

Decimus said nothing in reply, but led Ruma back through the courtyard to the hole.

'We're going up to the tower now?' the Etrurian prompted.

'There's nowhere else *to* go!' said Decimus, wearily. 'We've explored every room – the entire fort is a mystery! The tower is the only place left!'

'Well, if I'm going with you, I think I have a right to know what you're planning to do. Come on, Decimus, I want to *help* here – I'm trying to make up for all that bad stuff I did!'

'The White Snake,' Decimus said, but this time he let out a resigned sigh. 'We get it, we send Doom a message that we've got it and we exchange it for the others.'

Ruma paused for a moment. 'He'll snatch us the second we come out of the fort.'

'Ah . . . that's the clever bit.' Decimus grinned. 'We're not *leaving* the fort.'

Ruma looked confused, but he asked no more questions.

They retraced their steps past the slime, but this time Decimus was less careful and he accidentally brushed against the wall.

'Agrgh!' He rubbed frantically at his arm, but if anything the red patch that had sprouted up actually deepened. 'It feels like I'm on fire!'

The pain intensified, and didn't shift even when Ruma splashed him with a handful of water he'd found inside a small rock pool.

Decimus refused all further offers of help

from the Etrurian, however, and decided to carry on with the mission.

'I barely *touched* that stuff,' he said, starting up the steps once again. 'Can you imagine what would have happened if I'd fallen *against* it?'

Ruma shuddered, and increased his pace.

Finally, after more than a thousand steps (to Ruma's reckoning) they arrived at a heavy wooden door. As Decimus approached it, however, something incredible and terrifying happened with lightning speed. One second the young gladiator was reaching for the handle, the next he was staggering backwards … covered from head to toe in writhing green snakes. They had dropped from the ceiling in a grim tangle, forming a net that locked around Decimus, choking and twisting all around him.

Ruma shot a glance upwards, and another

three of the reptiles dropped from the roof of the tunnel on to *his* shoulders.

The two companions exploded into a mad panic, trying desperately to shake off the attacking creatures and slide from their tightening grasps.

Decimus slashed at his arms with the sword, his blade biting into one of the snakes. The reptile immediately let out a furious hiss and bit down on what it must have assumed to be Decimus's arm but was in fact another snake. This mistake caused the rest of the snakes to attack each other, as Decimus madly wriggled out from the tangle with only one or two fang-marks in his arms and legs.

Further back along the corridor, Ruma was having considerably more luck. The scrawny

Etrurian had adopted the tactic of remaining absolutely still and, remarkably, the snakes were curling down his body and slithering off into the shadows. Within a few seconds, he was left alone, shaken but very, very relieved.

The two friends hopped and jumped around the fighting snakes and returned to the door.

'We need to be more careful,' Ruma pointed out. 'Those things could have killed us . . .'

Decimus nodded and leaned his shoulder against the entrance, but it needed both of them pushing at full strength before it made even the slightest movement.

When the door *did* shift half an inch, Ruma moved back several paces and then charged at it. The resulting crash forced the opening to widen, and a wash of morning light spilled out into the corridor.

Decimus took one look at the small room in which they now found themselves, and frowned.

Apart from four more statues and a great window that looked out over the Rock toward Doom's ship, there was precious little else here. The noise of the army going about their morning routine was quite apparent.

Ruma padded over to the window, and peered outside.

'Doom is down there,' he said. 'He must have guessed where we were headed.'

'Can you see Gladius and the others?'

'No, but Groach is there. You can spot that *thing* from half a mile away.'

Decimus nodded in agreement, and began to study the room in greater detail.

'This is *too* odd,' Ruma muttered. 'I don't like it – not one b—'

The Etrurian had stopped speaking and was frozen to the spot. He was glancing curiously at an alcove in the wall opposite the window. Decimus found he had to move a little way through the room before he could follow Ruma's gaze, but when he did see what had attracted his friend he quickly adopted the same intrigued stare.

There, inside the alcove, was a large wooden box daubed with several strange symbols. Decimus knew the language they portrayed was similar to that he'd seen inscribed on the walls of the Winter Palace, but he had no idea what the message actually said.

He stepped over to the box and carefully raised his sword until the edge was positioned right underneath the lid. Then, instructing Ruma to move close to the other side of the niche, he began to raise the lid.

Ruma inched forward, and they both peered inside.

The interior of the box was, unexpectedly, empty. There was some straw in the bottom, and the skeleton of what appeared to be a small rodent, but otherwise nothing else.

Ruma leaned in closer, snatched hold of the lid and actually lifted it off. It rolled on to the floor when he dropped it, clattering loudly.

'Be careful,' Decimus warned, as the Etrurian actually put a hand into the box and began to rummage through the straw at the

bottom, but he should have paid greater

attention to his own words. Indeed, he'd become

so engrossed in Ruma's search that he failed to see a long, fat snake slither down from the top of the alcove and poise itself to strike.

There was a split-second hiss, and then the reptile darted forward.

Decimus staggered slightly, and dropped his sword. A sharp pain erupted in his neck: the bite had happened so quickly that the young gladiator found it hard to believe he had actually been bitten.

Ruma lunged forward and hacked at the snake, which was now fully uncoiling from the alcove: it was absolutely huge.

As soon as his sword found the creature's scaly flesh, it sprang sideways, curling quickly up the blade. In fact, the snake's lower body was so strong that it was supporting itself and rising up at the same time, a slimy mass of fury poised to strike.

Ruma tried to shake the sword, but the snake simply slithered over the blade, wound along his arm and began to tighten around his neck.

The Etrurian spat out a mouthful of saliva as he felt his throat become constricted.

On the other side of the room, Decimus was apparently recovering from a dizziness that had made him fall over each time he got up. Whatever effect the bite had had on his system, however, he still felt enough control to snatch up his sword and scramble across the floor towards Ruma.

Decimus winced, as the room swam around in his vision.

He reached the Etrurian just as the snake overcame him: Ruma writhed on the floor, his eyes bulging and his face turning as white as the creature now fastened tightly around his neck.

Screaming with rage, Decimus dropped his sword and instead made several grabs for the reptile's head. The snake was possessed of lightning speed, however, and it bit him again.

Once.

Twice.

Three times.

Decimus could now see very little, but he DID finally clamp a single hand on the snake's wide, flat head.

Driving the reptile down on to the floor, he knelt on its head and snatched up his sword.

Sensing the danger it now faced, the snake quickly uncoiled from Ruma and wrapped its length around Decimus, swiftly tightening around his arms, neck and chest.

Everything was happening so fast.

Roaring with anger and determination, Decimus fought to ignore the crushing pain now wracking his body. Feeling as though he was wading through quicksand, the young gladiator pushed forward, calling upon as much strength as he had left . . . and began to saw through the scaly flesh behind the snake's head.

The creature gave a sickening hiss and thrashed around wildly, its flailing tail-end whipping Ruma in the face and causing him to cry out in pain.

A spray of green liquid suddenly exploded from the snake as Decimus finally severed its head, splattering the walls in the process.

Two small blotches hit Ruma's sword, and the Etrurian gasped as the blade began to smoke. He quickly dropped the weapon and scrambled to his feet.

The snake writhed several times, but its movements were now slow and vague. At length, it became completely still.

'Th-that green stuff looks like the slime on the walls in the sewer tunnel,' Ruma panted. 'It burned right through my sword!'

'Get the snake on to my shoulders,' said Decimus, with a heavy sigh. He was still feeling woozy from the effects of the bite – if anything, the pain was intensifying. 'Preferably the end *without* all the blood: I don't want Doom to know that it's dead.'

Between them, Ruma and Decimus managed to support three quarters of the length of the White Snake and carry the creature to the window.

Far below, at the doors of the fort, Doom had gathered a group of his guards around him. Groach towered over them, his vein-riddled arms folded and his black mask gleaming in the morning sunlight.

'SLAVIOUS DOOM!' the young gladiator screamed. 'Hear me now – or pine for your lost treasure until the day you die!'

The overlord looked up at the top of the tower, his henchmen quickly joined by the larger army gathered around him.

'As you can see from where you stand, I now have your prize in *MY* possession. If you EVER wish to share that boast, you will do exactly as I say.'

Most of Doom's guards suppressed fits of quiet laughter, but the overlord himself showed no sign of amusement. He folded his arms defiantly and shouted back: 'Groach will execute your friends BEFORE your very ey—'

'And if he does, I will destroy the snake.'

Suddenly, Doom's face became a mask of absolute horror, and he held up both hands in a gesture that almost looked as though he was afraid.

'You must NOT do that, boy! No matter what happens, you must NEVER do that! If the White Snake dies . . . something absolutely terrible will happen.'

Decimus hid the puzzlement he felt at the pleading edge in the overlord's voice, and continued:

'Release ALL of my friends and have them brought to the fort doors, at once. Afterwards,

you will retreat to your ship. Then – and only
then – will I lower the snake on to the rocks in a
box. You will be free to collect it at will, and my
friends and I will be safe from you inside ...

Ruma frowned, and glanced over at Decimus, who had staggered slightly, and was beginning to twitch. Several of the snakebites now stood out on the young gladiator's neck, and he didn't look quite himself. Moreover, he was almost buckling under the weight of the dead reptile; sweat glistened on his shoulders.

Ruma shook himself free of the snake and made a grab for his friend, just as he collapsed.

Decimus lost consciousness with remarkable speed, caving under the reptile's weight, so that Ruma actually had to heave the creature off him in order to check he was still breathing.

'Decimus? Decimus!' the Etrurian cried frantically, as Doom's men began to shout commands at each other in the distance. 'Decimus! Please answer me!'

The young gladiator remained deathly still, but as Ruma glanced up again he saw that several other things in the room were far from motionless.

The statues in the middle of the chamber were slowly coming to life...

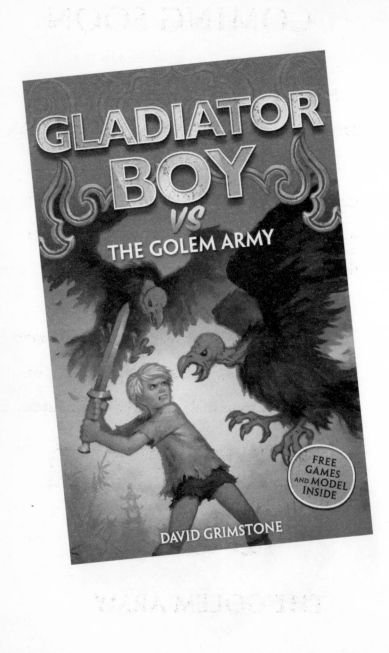

GLADIATOR BOY

vs

THE GOLEM ARMY

FREE GAMES AND MODEL INSIDE

DAVID GRIMSTONE

COMING SOON

Having killed the legendary White Snake,
Decimus Rex has accidentally unleashed a terrible
curse on Pin Yon Rock. However, as the young
gladiator lies poisoned at the top of the fort, it is
not quite clear whether the curse will be bad for
the slaves . . . or for Slavious Doom.

Will the boys finally wreak their revenge upon
the overlord and his grotesque apprentice . . . or
will this prove to be their last stand? Find out in . . .

THE GOLEM ARMY

GLADIATOR GAME
SIEGE!

In the following game, one player takes control of an army besieging a fort and the other plays the part of the defending inhabitants.

Randomly decide who plays who. The first player (the army) closes their eyes and stabs a pencil into Grid A. The result will tell both players a) how many days the army will have to end the siege and b) how many people are inside.

Then, taking it in turns, each player stabs a pencil at Grid B. Each result will tell the players how many days have passed and how many defenders have died.

If the days expire before the defenders are all dead, the DEFENDING player wins. If the defenders all die before the last day is spent, the ATTACKING player wins.

Have fun, and good luck!

GRID A

D – Days left   P – People Inside

D20-P20	D5-P10	D10-P5	D12-P15	D15-P12	D5-P10	D20-P20
D10-P10	D10-P5	D5-P10	D15-P12	D12-P15	D10-P5	D10-P10
D30-P30	D8-P4	D4-P8	D23-P12	D12-P23	D11-P18	D30-P30
D50-P50	D4-P8	D8-P4	D12-P23	D23-P12	D18-P11	D50-P50
D40-P40	D19-P8	D8-P19	D23-P12	D12-P23	D11-P18	D40-P40
D50-P50	D4-P8	D8-P4	D12-P23	D23-P12	D18-P11	D50-P50
D40-P40	D19-P8	D8-P19	D23-P12	D12-P23	D11-P18	D40-P40
D20-P20	D5-P10	D24-P5	D12-P15	D15-P12	D5-P10	D20-P20
D10-P10	D10-P5	D5-P24	D15-P12	D12-P15	D10-P5	D10-P10
D30-P30	D8-P4	D4-P8	D23-P12	D12-P23	D11-P18	D30-P30
D50-P50	D4-P8	D8-P4	D12-P23	D23-P12	D18-P11	D50-P50
D20-P20	D5-P10	D10-P5	D12-P15	D15-P12	D5-P10	D20-P20
D10-P10	D10-P5	D5-P10	D15-P12	D12-P15	D10-P5	D10-P10
D30-P30	D8-P4	D4-P8	D23-P12	D12-P23	D11-P18	D30-P30
D40-P40	D19-P8	D8-P19	D23-P12	D12-P23	D11-P18	D40-P40
D20-P20	D5-P10	D10-P5	D12-P15	D15-P12	D5-P10	D20-P20
D10-P10	D10-P5	D5-P10	D15-P12	D12-P15	D10-P5	D10-P10
D20-P20	D5-P10	D10-P5	D12-P15	D15-P12	D5-P10	D20-P20
D10-P10	D10-P5	D5-P10	D15-P12	D12-P15	D10-P5	D10-P10
D30-P30	D8-P4	D4-P8	D23-P12	D12-P23	D11-P18	D30-P30
D20-P20	D5-P10	D10-P5	D12-P15	D15-P12	D5-P10	D20-P20
D10-P10	D10-P5	D5-P10	D15-P12	D12-P15	D10-P5	D10-P10
D20-P20	D5-P10	D10-P5	D12-P15	D15-P12	D5-P10	D20-P20
D10-P10	D10-P5	D5-P10	D15-P12	D12-P15	D10-P5	D10-P10

GRID B

D – Days gone   P – People gone

D2-P2	D4-P4	D1-P1	D3-P3	D5-P5	D7-P7	D6-P6	D8-P8
D2-P2	D4-P4	D1-P1	D3-P3	D5-P5	D7-P7	D6-P6	D8-P8
D5-P5	D10-P5	D5-P10	D10-P5	D5-P10	D10-P5	D5-P10	D5-P5
D4-P4	D6-P12	D12-P6	D6-P12	D12-P6	D6-P12	D12-P6	D4-P4
D5-P5	D10-P5	D5-P10	D10-P5	D5-P10	D10-P5	D5-P10	D5-P5
D2-P2	D4-P4	D1-P1	D3-P3	D5-P5	D7-P7	D6-P6	D8-P8
D2-P2	D4-P4	D1-P1	D3-P3	D5-P5	D7-P7	D6-P6	D8-P8
D5-P5	D10-P5	D5-P10	D10-P5	D5-P10	D10-P5	D5-P10	D5-P5
D4-P4	D6-P12	D12-P6	D6-P12	D12-P6	D6-P12	D12-P6	D4-P4
D5-P5	D10-P5	D5-P10	D10-P5	D5-P10	D10-P5	D5-P10	D5-P5
D2-P2	D4-P4	D1-P1	D3-P3	D5-P5	D7-P7	D6-P6	D8-P8
D5-P5	D10-P5	D5-P10	D10-P5	D5-P10	D10-P5	D5-P10	D5-P5
D4-P4	D6-P12	D12-P6	D6-P12	D12-P6	D6-P12	D12-P6	D4-P4
D5-P5	D10-P5	D5-P10	D10-P5	D5-P10	D10-P5	D5-P10	D5-P5
D2-P2	D4-P4	D1-P1	D3-P3	D5-P5	D7-P7	D6-P6	D8-P8
D5-P5	D10-P5	D5-P10	D10-P5	D5-P10	D10-P5	D5-P10	D5-P5
D4-P4	D6-P12	D12-P6	D6-P12	D12-P6	D6-P12	D12-P6	D4-P4
D5-P5	D10-P5	D5-P10	D10-P5	D5-P10	D10-P5	D5-P10	D5-P5
D2-P2	D4-P4	D1-P1	D3-P3	D5-P5	D7-P7	D6-P6	D8-P8
D5-P5	D10-P5	D5-P10	D10-P5	D5-P10	D10-P5	D5-P10	D5-P5
D4-P4	D6-P12	D12-P6	D6-P12	D12-P6	D6-P12	D12-P6	D4-P4
D5-P5	D10-P5	D5-P10	D10-P5	D5-P10	D10-P5	D5-P10	D5-P5
D2-P2	D4-P4	D1-P1	D3-P3	D5-P5	D7-P7	D6-P6	D8-P8

CHARACTER PROFILE
GROACH

NAME: Groach (real name unknown)

FROM: Campania, Italy

HEIGHT: 2.47 metres

BODY TYPE: Muscular, grotesque

GROACH QUIZ: How well do you know Groach? Can you answer the following questions?

1. WHO IS THE FIRST PERSON TO SEE GROACH IN THE GROUNDS OF THE WINTER PALACE?

2. WHICH TWO SLAVES COME TO BLOWS WITH EACH OTHER IN THIS BOOK?

3. WHICH SLAVE ALMOST KNOCKS GROACH OUT WITH A MACE?

GLADIATOR BOY

WWW.GLADIATORBOY.COM

Have you checked out the Gladiator Boy website? It's the place to go for games, downloads, activities, sneak previews and lots of fun!

Sign up to the newsletter at **WWW.GLADIATORBOY.COM** and receive exclusive extra content and the opportunity to enter special members-only competitions.